The DINOSAUR
DEPARTMENT STORE

Written by Lily Murray

Illustrated by Richard Merritt

Edited by Hannah Daffern and Helen Brown

Designed by Zoe Bradley and Angie Allison

Cover design by John Bigwood

For Eliza Jane — LM

For Thomas David — RM

Buster Books

Eliza Jane was an **unusual** child.
Some called her wilful, some called her **wild!**

She didn't like **bedtime** or **broccoli** or **rules**,
Nor tidying up, nor going to school.

So it didn't come as a **great** surprise
when, on her birthday, Eliza Jane cried,

"Mummy! Daddy! Now that I'm four,
I'd like you to buy me a **real dinosaur!**"

Her parents weren't keen, it has to be said,

They **wished** she had asked for a **rabbit** instead.

But they swallowed their fears, put on a brave face.

"Let's go," said Mummy. "I know **just** the right place."

"Hooray! Hooray!" said Eliza Jane,
And off they went on the 10:20 train.

They rushed from the station
to the grand front door,

Of the one and only
Dinosaur Store.

DINOSAUR
DEPARTMENT STORE

They rang the bell.
The door opened
wide.
Eliza Jane stepped
boldly
inside.

They were met
by a man
in a
long
velvet cloak,

Who twirled
his moustache
and
smiled
as he spoke.

"Mr Magisaurus, here at your service.
Welcome, my dears! No need to be nervous.

Come with me on my **magical** tour
of the dazzling

Dinosaur Department Store!"

He pulled back the curtain with outrageous flair.
ROARS and HISSES zipped through the air.

DINOSAURS

"So much to see, it'll make your heads spin.
Are you ready, dear friends?
Then let us begin!"

"We have **huge** ones,
scaly ones, dinos with **beaks**,
Sweet little fluffy ones,

SQUEAK!
SQUEAK!
SQUEAK!

Fang-toothed carnivores **grinding** their jaws,
Rip-roaring raptors with **sharp, slashing** claws.

Honking Hadrosaurs playing in herds,

Tiny feathered theropods
squawking
like birds.

A Plesiosaurus **feasting** on fish,

YIKES

Spinosaurus!

Give that one a miss.

Huge stomping sauropods **stretching** their necks,
Bigger than houses, the gentlest of pets.

Amargasaurus with her mighty sail,
A colossal Diplodocus **whipping** his tail.

These are Ankylosaurs, **armoured** like tanks.
One's called Maud, the
other's called Frank.

A clever, fierce Troodon
who stays up
all night ...

... and Ms Tyrannosaurus
with her **bone-crunching bite!**"

Mr Magisaurus turned to the crowd.

He **simpered** and **smirked** and looked very proud.

"At last we have reached the end of the tour.

It's time to choose your **own** dinosaur!"

But Eliza Jane had turned to go.

"Thank you," she said, "but my answer is NO.

I did enjoy your **wonderful** tour,

But I no longer want a **real** dinosaur."

Mr Magisaurus cried out in dismay,
"YOU'VE WASTED MY TIME.
GET OUT OF MY WAY!"

Eliza Jane's parents were **rocked** to the core,
As the storekeeper **flung** them straight out the door.

Plesiosaurus
(ple-si-oh-sore-us)

Raptors
(rap-tores)

Hadrosaurs
(had-roe-sores)

Theropods
(therra-pods)

Spinosaurus
(spy-nuh-sore-us)

Sauropods
(sore-oh-pods)

Amargasaurus
(ah-mar-gah-sore-us)

Diplodocus
(dip-plod-oh-kus)

Ankylosaurs
(an-kie-loh-sores)

Troodon
(troe-oh-don)

Tyrannosaurus
(tie-ran-oh-sore-us)

First published in Great Britain in 2019 by Buster Books,
an imprint of Michael O'Mara Books Limited, 9 Lion Yard, Tremadoc Road, London SW4 7NQ

W www.mombooks.com/buster   f Buster Books   ✚ @BusterBooks

Text © 2019 Lily Murray
Illustrations © 2019 Richard Merritt
Layout and design © 2019 Buster Books

ISBN: 978-1-78055-596-6

6 8 10 9 7

This book was printed in October 2019 by Leo Paper Products Ltd, Heshan Astros Printing Limited,
Xuantan Temple Industrial Zone, Gulao Town, Heshan City, Guangdong Province, China.